DATE DUE			
SEP 1	NOV 01	OCT 26	FEB 04
OCT 20		DEC 13	APR 13
JAN 29	15	JAN 08	NOV 30
MAR 22	DEC 18	JAN 2	
	JAN 25	JAN 30	FEB 14 2008
APR 10	FEB 16		FEB 05
	MAR 14	FEB 12	APR 19
SEP 14 2000	APR 10	APR 08	
OCT 05 2000	MAY 19	APR 23	
OCT 13	MAY 10	DEC 04	
OCT 1	OCT 15	DEC 17	

E
591.77   Owens, Caleb
89
OWE   Coral reefs

                              $15.95

Fieldcrest South Elem Lib

Coral Reefs

Coral Reefs

Caleb Owens

THE CHILD'S WORLD®, INC.

Library of Congress Cataloging-in-Publication Data
Owens, Caleb.
Coral reefs / by Caleb Owens.
p.   cm.
Includes index.
Summary: A brief introduction to coral reefs
and the animals and plants that live there.
ISBN 1-56766-467-9 (lib. reinforced … alk. paper)
1. Coral reef animals—Juvenile literature.
2. Coral reefs and islands—Juvenile literature.   [1. Coral reefs and islands.]   I. Title.
QL125.O84   1998
591.77'89—dc21   97-30407
                                        CIP
                                        AC

Photo Credits

© Charles Seaborne/Tony Stone Images: 2, 13
© Chuck Davis/Tony Stone Images: 23
© Darryl Torckler/Tony Stone Images: 20
© Franklin J. Viola/Comstock, Inc.: cover, 10, 30
© Marilyn Kazmers/Sharksong: 9, 29
© Marilyn Kazmers/Sharksong/Dembinsky Photo Assoc. Inc.: 19, 26,
© Mark J. Thomas/Dembinsky Photo Assoc. Inc.: 15
© Paul Chesley/Tony Stone Images: 16
© Robert and Linda Mitchell: 24
© 1997 Susan Blanche/Dembinsky Photo Assoc. Inc.: 6

On the cover...

Front cover: Some bright fish are swimming past this coral reef near the island of Fiji.
Page 2: This colorful coral reef is in the western Pacific Ocean.

Table of Contents

Welcome to the Coral Reef!

Imagine a weird world in which strange creatures live and play. Some creatures float by on eight legs. Others look like giant fans. In this strange place, horses move without legs, and cucumbers crawl on the floor.

All these weird creatures live near tall orange and green buildings. But the strangest part of all is that the buildings are alive! What kind of place is this? It's a coral reef.

⇐ This *parrot fish* is swimming near many types of coral.

What Is a Coral Reef?

Coral reefs are made by strange animals called **coral polyps**. Coral polyps are about the size of your fingernail. They have soft bodies and wavy arms, or **tentacles**, that bring food to their mouths. To protect their soft bodies, coral polyps make rocky cups. They use the rocky cups as protective homes.

These coral polyps are reaching out with their tentacles to feed. ⇒

When a coral polyp dies, another coral polyp builds its cup house on top of the old one. Slowly, the polyps form a pile of tiny cups. Over time, the piles of polyp houses grow higher and bigger. They form what we call a coral reef. Coral reefs grow slowly. Many large reefs are thousands of years old!

What Do Coral Reefs Look Like?

Coral reefs look like huge rock gardens. They are covered with lots of shapes, from long tubes to flat plates. They also are very colorful. Coral reefs can be deep green, bright red, or even gold.

The largest coral reef in the world is the *Great Barrier Reef*. This reef is near the country of Australia. It is over 1,200 miles long! If all the coral reefs in the world were put together, they would be bigger than Asia, Africa, Europe, Antarctica, and North America combined!

This coral reef is full of many different shapes and colors. ⇒

Where Do Coral Reefs Grow?

Coral reefs are found only in the ocean waters near the **equator**. The equator is an imaginary line around the middle of Earth. Near the equator, the weather is always warm. The ocean there is warm, too. Coral polyps cannot live in cold water. The warm waters near the equator are the only places they can live.

This coral reef is growing in the warm waters near New Guinea. ⇒

Are There Different Types of Reefs?

When different kinds of coral grow together, they make different types of reefs. There are three main types. *Fringe reefs* are attached to the shore and grow faster than other reefs. They can completely circle a small island. *Barrier reefs* are the largest. They form just off the coast of land areas and make a barrier between the land and the ocean.

Atoll reefs are the strangest of all. They began long ago as fringe reefs around small volcanoes. But over thousands of years, each volcano sank into the sea and disappeared. Now all that is left is the coral reef circle with nothing in the middle!

⇐ It is easy to see how big the *Great Barrier Reef* really is.

What Kinds of Fish Live in Coral Reefs?

Coral reefs make great hiding places for fish. Divers often see thousands of fish swimming in and around a reef. There are strange-looking fish such as *sea horses* and *triggerfish*. There are dangerous fish such as *sharks* and *moray eels*. There are also thousands of very beautiful fish, such as *angelfish*. All of these fish find food and safety in coral reefs.

This colorful *angelfish* is swimming near a coral reef. ⇒

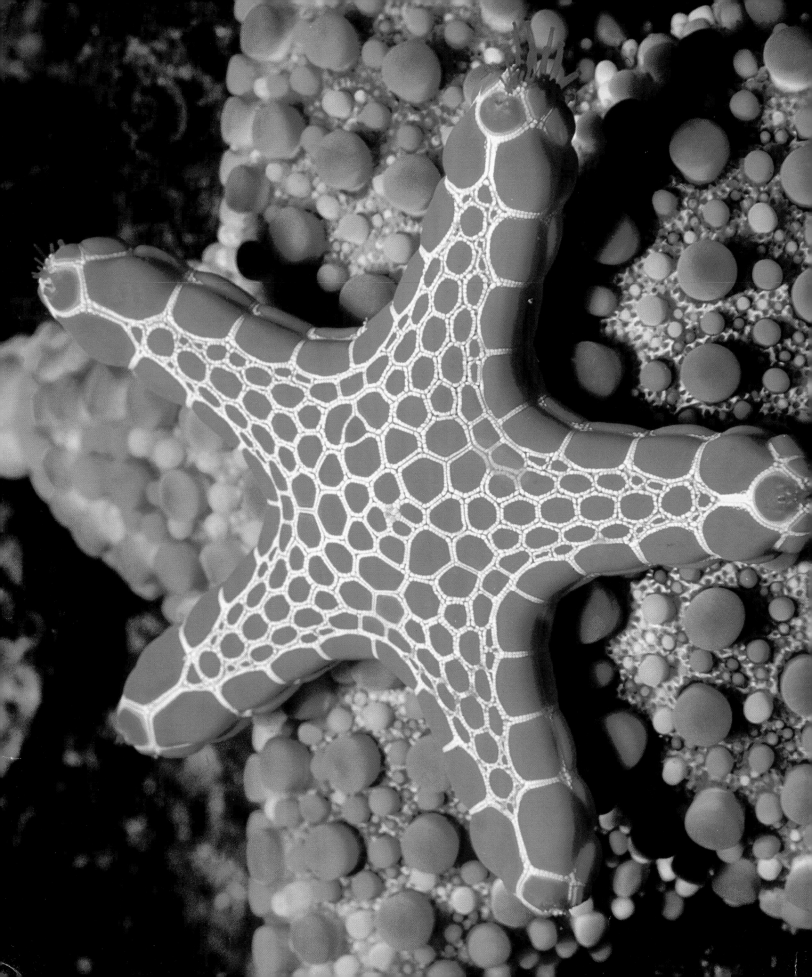

What Other Animals Live in Reefs?

Besides fish, many other strange creatures live in coral reefs. The eight-tentacled *octopus* likes to hide in dark places. Huge *giant clams* love to face the sunlight when it shines through the water. And colorful *starfish* often rest along the reef's steep sides. In a coral reef, there are strange and beautiful creatures everywhere.

⇐ This bright red *starfish* is resting on top of another one.

Many creatures that live in coral reefs look a lot like plants. This helps them to hide and to sneak up on their food. The *sea cucumber* and the *sea anemone* (SEE uh–NEH–muh–nee) are two such creatures. They both use their wavy tentacles to attract fish. When a fish touches the tentacles, poison comes out. The poison makes the fish unable to move. After a short time, the cucumber or the anemone can eat the fish without worrying about it swimming away.

This *sea anemone* is waving its tentacles to attract fish. ⇒

Do Coral Reef Animals Get Along?

Since sea cucumbers and sea anemones are so dangerous, many animals leave them alone. But the *clown fish* actually lives in the tentacles of the sea anemone! The clown fish's slimy skin protects it from the stinging tentacles.

The clown fish and the sea anemone help each other. The fish protects the anemone from **predators**, or enemies that would try to eat it. In return, the clown fish lives safely in the anemone's dangerous tentacles. This kind of cooperation is called **symbiosis**. Many other reef animals use symbiosis to stay alive. It is one of the things that makes coral reefs so special.

⇐ These *clown fish* are swimming safely near an anemone.

Coral reefs are easily destroyed. Strong hurricanes and other storms sometimes sweep away large parts of reefs. Pollution from cities and boats can harm the water and the reef's animals. And some animals destroy coral reefs by eating them. The *crown-of-thorns sea star* eats the tiny coral polyps. Without the polyps, the reef cannot keep growing. Another animal called the *parrot fish* scrapes away the hard coral with its strong mouth.

⇐ This *crown-of-thorns sea star* is feeding on a large area of coral. 27

The biggest danger to coral reefs, though, is people. Boats and anchors break off chunks of reef when they float by. Trash and waste destroy the reef's beautiful plants and animals. And some swimmers even take pieces of coral reefs home as gifts or decorations.

This chain from a boat anchor is destroying part of a coral reef. ⇒

The best way to keep coral reefs safe is to leave them alone. Keeping boats and other machines away helps protect the tall coral. And keeping the ocean clean helps the reef's animals stay healthy and happy. If we take care of our coral reefs today, we will be able to enjoy them for years to come.

⇐ Coral reefs like this one are full of life.

Glossary

coral polyps (KOR–ull PAH–lips)
Coral polyps are tiny animals that build coral reefs. The reefs are made up of the little rocky cups the polyps call home.

equator (ee–KWAY–ter)
The equator is an imaginary line around the middle of Earth. Coral reefs grow in the warm waters near the equator.

predator (PREH–duh–ter)
A predator is an animal that hunts and eats other animals. Many predators live in coral reefs.

symbiosis (sim–bee–OH–sis)
When animals help each other and cooperate, it is called symbiosis. The clown fish and the sea anemone use symbiosis to stay alive.

tentacles (TEN–tuh–culz)
Tentacles are long, wavy, armlike body parts. Some animals have very poisonous tentacles.

Index